GIRLS SURVIVE

Girls Survive is published by Stone Arch Books, an imprint of Capstone.
1710 Roe Crest Drive
North Mankato, Minnesota 56003
www.capstonepub.com

Library of Congress Cataloging-in-Publication Data is available on the Library of
Congress website.

ISBN: 978-1-4965-9690-1 (hardcover)
ISBN: 978-1-4965-9910-0 (paperback)
ISBN: 978-1-4965-9761-8 (eBook PDF)

Summary: The American Revolution is raging in Philadelphia, and Rebecca
is determined to do all she can to help. With her father stationed with George
Washington's army at nearby Whitemarsh, it's up to Rebecca to help her mother
at home with her younger siblings. When Rebecca intercepts a message about an
impending British attack against the Patriots, she knows she has to act. It's up to her
to get the message to the Patriot army—before it's too late.

Image Credits:
Shutterstock: Aliona Manakova, design element,
Spalnic, (watercolor) design element throughout

Cover art by Jane Pica

Designer: Kayla Rossow

Printed and bound in the USA.
PA3342

REBECCA
RIDES FOR FREEDOM

An American Revolution Survival Story

by Emma Carlson Berne
illustrated by Francesca Ficorilli

STONE ARCH BOOKS
a capstone imprint

CHAPTER ONE

Philadelphia, Pennsylvania
December 2, 1777
6:00 a.m.

I could hear baby Henry crying before I opened my eyes. The icy cold pressed on the quilt drawn up around my nose, and I huddled close to my younger brother Benjamin's warm, sleeping body.

I squeezed my eyes shut, but after just a second, I opened them again. In the same motion, I flung back the quilt. Mother needed me. Henry had been sick for a week now, and by the sound of the crying downstairs, he was no better this morning.

In the bed, Benjamin mumbled something and reached for the quilts. I drew them up under his chin and tucked them in. "Stay under the covers until I build a fire," I murmured to him.

I smoothed back my brother's brown hair and studied his face. It was pale against the white sheets, and his cheekbones stood out in sharp points.

We'd been spooning less and less cornmeal into our bowls since Father left in November to join his regiment. They were stationed at Whitemarsh, about thirteen miles away from our home in northern Philadelphia. Benjamin was beginning to show the effects of our meager diet.

I pulled my blue woolen dress over the long, white shift I wore to bed and quickly pinned my hair back under my white cap. Then I climbed down the rough ladder that led from the loft where Benjamin and I slept to the lower level.

I hurried over to Mother, who sat by the cold fireplace. Her hair was still in its nighttime braid. Outside the window, the pale winter dawn glinted off the snow that reached almost to the bottom of the sill.

"Let me have him, Mother. You go get dressed," I said.

I took Henry from Mother's arms. As soon as I laid my hands on him, I could feel the fever burning off him in waves. I bent my head and kissed his forehead. Immediately, I could feel the heat of the fever on my lips.

I pulled back and looked down at my baby brother. Henry's little face was red, and his mouth parted with his noisy breathing. His blue eyes were glazed. This morning, they didn't search for my face.

"He became worse in the night," Mother said. She came back out of the bedroom with her wool dress on and a gray shawl over her shoulders. She took Henry back, her face creased with worry.

I began laying logs in the fireplace as Mother talked on behind me. "He's terribly sick. If we

should lose him . . . and your father not here . . . Rebecca, I don't know if I can keep going."

Her voice suddenly filled with tears.

I jumped up and put an arm around Mother's shoulders. I had never witnessed her crying—not even the day Benjamin had been bitten by the copperhead.

For weeks now our family had been waiting and waiting for news from Whitemarsh, where Father's regiment was stationed with General Washington. General Howe and the Redcoats would surely attack—but when? No one knew.

We'd been waiting and waiting, and nerves were fraying thin. Now, with Henry sick and the cornmeal so low in the barrel, I knew Mother was almost to the end of her strength.

"All will be well, Mother," I said, knowing the words meant nothing. "I'll make the pudding this morning. You sit with Henry."

I blew up the fire and set the pot on the iron stand in the big, open fireplace. As I stirred, I thought of the big, aching hole that Father's absence had caused in our family.

It wasn't just the chores, though it was true that we struggled to chop enough wood just to heat the kitchen. It wasn't just the money either—Father had been forced to close the blacksmith shop in the barn when he marched away with General Washington.

The house just seemed darker and chillier without Father's big smile and big beard and big boots drying by the fire every night. Everything seemed thin and desperate.

I stared into the bubbling corn mush, squeezing the iron ladle tightly in my hand. I couldn't just let this dark, cold feeling overtake us. I had to do something. I had to. Father would be counting on me.

After breakfast, Mother rocked Henry in the cradle, trying to hush his poor little wails, and I escaped to the barn. I breathed a sigh of relief as I pushed open the heavy wooden door. The smell of hay and cows and horses was heavy, and I inhaled it like perfume.

Halfway down the aisle, my bay horse, Brownie, flopped his head up and down over the half-door of his stall. His tether rope hung loose from his halter.

"Did you untie the knot again?" I scolded as I slipped into the stall. I ran my hands over Brownie's arched neck, then smoothed his long, black mane.

Brownie had been my very own horse since I was six years old. Father had trained him and given him to me on my birthday. Brownie and I understood each other. I always felt better when I was leaning against his side, as I was now, my

cheek against his sleek brown coat. I could hear his
massive heart beating deep within his body.

A gust of icy air whirled in as Benjamin pushed
the barn door open. His hair still stuck up on his
head from the night.

"There wasn't much pudding this morning,"
he said, taking a bucket from the corner. He started
sprinkling corn for the chickens, who spent the
winter in the barn aisle. They clucked hysterically,
stabbing the dirt floor with their beaks.

"You know there's hardly any meal left in
the barrel," I said. I retied Brownie's tether in the
clove hitch—the only knot he couldn't untie—and
fastened his stall door behind me. "Until Father
comes back and opens the blacksmith shop, the only
money we have is what Mother and I can get selling
the vegetables."

For a few months now, Mother and I had been
forced to call on Redcoat officers in order to sell the

potatoes and carrots we'd harvested in the fall. But with Henry sick, I'd gone out by myself the past two weeks.

"But if Father is killed—" Benjamin said.

"Don't even say that!" I whirled around. "He won't be! He'll come back!"

Benjamin gazed at me with the same steady gaze he'd had since we were little. Even back then he never grew angry in a quarrel. He'd just watch me, as he was now, until my anger drained away. It was a trick I wished I could master.

"He will be back," I muttered. I grabbed the bucket and stool to start the milking, although Daisy was almost dry. Another thing to worry about.

"You can't know that," Benjamin insisted. "Look at Goody Cook. What if that happens to us?"

Goody Cook was our neighbor to the south. Her only male relative, her son, Daniel, had been killed at the Battle of Trenton. With no way to support herself, she'd been forced to sell her farm and go live with her sister in Germantown.

I thought of Father dead, Henry dead, the farm sold, Brownie and the other animals taken away by strangers. "No!" I cried out. "I'm not going to let that happen."

Benjamin looked almost like he wanted to laugh and cry at the same time. "How are you going to do that? We've got the Redcoat army against us!"

"I don't know how," I said stubbornly, opening Daisy's stall. "I just know I'm going to."

But as I crouched on the stool and pressed my head against Daisy's side, I wondered if Benjamin was right.

How am I going to save my family when the Redcoats are against us? I worried.

CHAPTER **TWO**

Mother was scrubbing out the breakfast bowls with a rag and water when Benjamin and I came back in.

"Rebecca, you'll have to sell the vegetables yourself this morning," she said. She gestured wearily at the wooden cradle where Henry lay asleep, his little chest rising and falling quickly. "He's just dropped off. Be sure to stop at the Bingham house. I heard new officers are stationed there now."

I nodded. Ever since Philadelphia had been taken over by the Redcoats, the officers had been living in the houses of the fine people in town. They didn't even ask; they just moved in. Sometimes they even turned the families out onto the street in the middle of the night.

Lydia Wright's baby sister had died that way. Lydia and her parents hadn't been able to find shelter for three hours. By then, the baby was dead of the cold.

Mother tightened her lips. "Remember, don't speak too much. We don't know that the Binghams aren't spies."

"I know." I tried to reassured her. "I won't, Mother."

No one knew quite what to make of Quakers, like the Binghams. They were a pious, tight-knit group. They refused to support the Patriot fight for American independence. But they weren't

Tories—they didn't support the side of King George either. They claimed to be neutral.

As Mother said, though, how could anyone really know? Some people thought the Quakers were Tory spies, though no one had been able to prove that.

I put on my mittens and heavy, red woolen cloak and pulled the cloak's hood close around my face. I dug through the barrel of damp sand where we kept the potatoes and carrots. The sand kept them from spoiling or sprouting over the winter.

When my basket was loaded, I braced myself, then opened the front door. Icy wind immediately swept into my face, scouring my skin with little bits of hard snow. The cold bit through the layers of wool I wore as if I were naked.

I bent my head and trudged the quarter mile to the Bingham house. When I finally arrived, I knocked at the back door.

"Hello, Rebecca," Mistress Bingham said as she opened the door. "Selling again, then?"

"Yes, mistress," I replied, stepping over the doorway into the steamy kitchen.

Something was bubbling in the pot on the range. A servant girl, her face hidden by her cap, was chopping turnips at the wide wooden table in the center of the kitchen.

"My mother says you have . . . guests," I continued, "so perhaps you would need more vegetables?"

The *guests* were there now. I could hear voices coming from behind the closed parlor door. Faintly, I could smell tobacco smoke.

"Yes, I do, and the officers are being fairly congenial," Mistress Bingham said, taking my basket and inspecting the carrots. "I'll take these." She laid most of the carrots to the side and pressed two small coins into my hand.

Just then, from somewhere near the front of the house, there was a small *bang!* and a scuffle. The parlor door across the hall flew open, and several officers rushed toward the noise.

"Rebecca, show yourself out," Mistress Bingham directed, flustered. "I should attend to this." With that, she hurried toward the door, leaving me alone with the servant girl, who had begun to calmly chop the carrots I had just brought.

I watched for a moment and then turned away, already thinking of pressing the coins into Mother's hand. Before I could make it to the door, though, the servant girl spoke up behind me.

"Your father's a Patriot soldier, isn't he?" she asked in a carrying voice.

I whirled around. "Shhh! How do you know?" The officers were outside, but I felt exposed just hearing the words aloud.

The girl regarded me from under her heavy brows. Her smooth, freckled face betrayed nothing. "I saw him marching out to Whitemarsh with the regiment. You blew him a kiss, and he caught it. But you don't want the mistress to know that, do you?"

I thought of denying it. But something—some honest impulse, maybe some reason just to talk about Father—stopped me. Instead I said, "Yes. He's at Whitemarsh with General Washington right now."

The minute the words were out of my mouth, I wished I could take them back. How could I be so foolish? I must be distracted by the strain of the morning. How else could I explain standing in a house full of Recoats, declaring to a stranger that my father was a Patriot?

Just then, Mistress Bingham's voice rang from the front of the house. "Betsy! I need you!"

The servant girl put down her knife. After giving me one last inscrutable look, she hurried out of the room.

I turned back toward the door. My basket still had some potatoes left in it, and Mother would be waiting for the money.

But as I reached for the door, a thought crossed my mind—I was *in* a house full of officers. And they were all gone, just for a moment. Maybe I could do a little careful looking around.

I felt my pulse quicken. Looking around was dangerous. But somehow, talking about Father made me feel bold—as if I had some of his bravery in me.

I swallowed hard and cast a glance around the room. Not much to see—the big wooden table in the middle of the room, the fireplace, bundles of dried corn and herbs that had been gathered in the summer hanging on the walls.

Tentatively, I lifted a cloth covering a bowl. Dough formed into a ball sat underneath. I lowered the cloth, feeling foolish.

What am I doing, poking around a kitchen when Mother sits at home, waiting? I scolded myself.

I turned to go when the half-open parlor door across the hall caught my eye. The men hadn't closed it all the way when they'd rushed out front. Through the open door, I could just catch a glimpse of a pigeon-hole desk stuffed with papers and a chair shoved back.

I swallowed hard. I could hear my heart pounding loudly in my ears. It was as if my body knew what I was going to do before my mind did.

I crept toward the kitchen doorway and paused. To the right, down the hall, was the open front door. I could hear the sounds of some kind of scuffling activity out front.

"And then it fired," someone was saying from outside.

Betsy's voice followed. "Lift your head, sir."

Someone's gun must have gone off accidentally, I realized. *They'll all be distracted.*

I fixed my eyes on the parlor doorway. Two steps would bring me out of the kitchen, across the hall, and into the parlor.

I took one step. The floorboard creaked loudly, and I froze, the blood pounding in my chest. My hands were chilly, and my face was covered in sweat.

Another step. One more and I was in the room. I gently eased the door closed behind me.

Not waiting to see if anyone had noticed, I hurried over to the desk and began rifling through the papers. Page after page of closely written correspondence. I was in a kind of fever, not even knowing what I was looking for.

Something slammed in the back regions of the house, and I jumped, dropping the papers in my hand. I had to get out of here.

But before I could leave, something caught my eye—a blob of red wax. It was sealing a letter that had been placed on the corner of the desk, away from the other papers.

Father's voice was suddenly in my mind. "The colors of the waxes mean different things, my little Becky," he explained.

It was as if I were with him again, on that hot summer day back at the beginning of the war. Bees buzzed lazily in and out of the window that had been propped open with a stick. Father sat at his own desk in our parlor. He held the letters ready for the post in his hand.

In my mind, he fanned them before me, his soft eyes smiling. His hands were stained, as they always were, from the soot of his blacksmith's forge.

"Black is for bad news. Blue is for victories. Red is always one officer to another." Father sighed and tucked the letters into a basket. "Soon, I'll be writing you letters, my dear."

"When you go away?" I asked.

Father nodded, his face clouding over. He drew me close to him and hugged me tightly. The memory was so vivid I could almost feel it.

Back in the parlor, the red seal seemed to glare up at me. *One officer to another.* That's what Father had said. That meant important.

I didn't wait to think further. With trembling fingers, I broke the seal and quickly scanned the letter. Words and phrases leaped out at me.

General Howe, I need your leave to give command for the movement of our troops . . . gather for the attack on the regiments at Whitemarsh . . . to commence at dawn on December the fourth . . . orders will be given to keep the utmost secrecy . . .

under no circumstances shall this attack be revealed, lest the enemy has time to prepare defenses. . . .

There was a roaring in my ears, coming from inside my head. Black dots floated in front of my eyes. It was like the time Tom Mason's filly had run away with me in the saddle. All I could do was hold on as the world rushed past.

These are the plans for Howe's attack on Whitemarsh! I realized. And not just any plans— specific times and dates.

I scanned the paper again. December fourth, at dawn. That's when they would attack. And today was—I thought back rapidly—today was December second! The attack would be the day after tomorrow—by sunup!

My hands were wet and hot as I realized the urgency of the situation. The paper trembled so much in my grasp that I could hear it rattling.

I had to do something—immediately. I folded
the letter back up, and just then, a thump sounded
in the hall outside the door.

My heart shot into my mouth. I tried to jam the
letter down the front of my dress, but it was too late.
The parlor door swung open.

CHAPTER **THREE**

Betsy stood in the doorway, a bucket in one hand and a bunch of rags in the other. Something pale pink dripped from the rags to the floor.

Neither of us moved. I could only guess at how I looked—red-faced and disheveled, poised over a desk strewn with papers, one of them poking out of the neck of my dress.

Betsy's eyes narrowed, and she moved into the room, swiftly kicking the door half closed behind her. She set down the bucket and rags and came over to me.

"Snooping, are you?" she said.

I swallowed hard. I could deny it. But who in the world would believe me? What else would I be doing in Mistress Bingham's parlor?

"Looking for money?" Betsy asked. "You'll find none here."

"Not money!" I burst out. "Please don't tell the mistress! It's my father's life!" Slowly, I drew the letter out from my dress. "It tells of an attack on Whitemarsh. My father is stationed there. If I can warn him, it could save his life. He could come home to us."

Some kind of a spasm went over Betsy's face. She didn't move. The room was utterly still. All I could hear was the light in and out of Betsy's breathing.

"Get out the back door right now," she suddenly ordered. "Mistress is in the front. An officer's gun went off by accident. He shot himself in the foot. They're all in the street still. The back way is clear."

I gaped at her. "You . . . you're helping me?" I asked. "But I thought you were on the side of the Tories!"

Betsy scowled. "What, just because I work for Mistress Bingham? I have a mind of my own, thank you very much." She paused. "My brother was beaten in the street when he wouldn't get out of the way of the Redcoats. They broke his arm."

"Oh! That's terrible!" I felt like I was in a dream. Things were changing so fast.

Betsy nodded, emotion written all over her face. "Now hurry. It won't take long for them to discover the dispatch is missing. I'll say I was cleaning and knocked the papers off."

In one movement, she swept her arm across the surface of the desk. All the papers fluttered to the floor. "I can say I jarred the desk too."

As I watched open-mouthed, Betsy calmly dumped a jar of ink over the jumbled papers on the floor.

"There," she said. "That's a right mess. By the time I explain and they sort out the papers, you'll be long gone."

"But . . . but you're taking all the blame on yourself," I protested. "You'll lose your place!"

Betsy shrugged, a little smile hovering around the corners of her mouth. "I may. But I don't think so. Mistress can't do without me."

Voices suddenly rose in the front hall, and Betsy's eyes darted to the door. "That's them!" she hissed. "Run!"

I grabbed Betsy's hand and squeezed it. "Thank you! I'll do this for my father—and your brother."

Betsy's face folded for a moment, as if she would cry, but then she pulled herself together. With another nod, she shoved me toward the door.

I crammed the dispatch all the way down my bodice and slipped out the open door, feeling as exposed as a deer in a meadow. The front entryway was crammed with the soldiers coming back in.

It took only seconds to move between the parlor door and the kitchen. Every instant I expected to hear a shout of, "Hey! Stop, girl!" from the front. But their attention was on one another.

I darted into the kitchen with my heart hammering in my ears. The large room was deserted. Only Betsy's stew bubbled over the range. The kitchen door, pushed by the breeze, swung a little on its hinges, creaking back and forth. The chilly air streamed in from outside, and the snowy ground shone brightly.

My hand was on the latch when a babble of voices rose from the parlor. "Stupid girl! Everything ruined!" someone shouted.

There was a smacking sound, and Betsy
cried out. I felt sick. I knew she was taking the
punishment I deserved.

Then another voice said, "Sir? The Howe
dispatch—I think it's missing."

I felt the blood drain from of my face. My
knees went weak. *How quickly they discovered it!*

I bolted from the kitchen door, running as
fast as I could over the frozen ground. The whole
time, I kept my hand pressed over the dispatch in
my bodice. If the soldiers were behind me, I never
paused to see.

CHAPTER FOUR

Philadelphia, Pennsylvania
December 2, 1777
10:25 a.m.

"Mother!" I shouted, bursting in the back door of the house. "Mother!"

Hearing my voice, Mother rushed from the parlor. Henry was in her arms and Benjamin was close behind.

"What? What is it?" she asked, her face alarmed.

I was breathing so hard I could hardly speak. I drew the crumpled dispatch from my bodice and handed it to my mother. Then I bent over and put my hands on my knees to catch my breath.

"'Attack on the regiments at Whitemarsh . . . ,'" Mother read. She looked at me in horror.

"Keep reading," I said. "There's more."

"'. . . to commence at dawn on December the fourth . . .'" Mother gasped. "Rebecca, these are secret orders from General Howe himself! Where did you find this?"

"At Mistress Bingham's." Quickly, I explained what had happened in the parlor, including Betsy's role in my escape. "I got out safely. Betsy said she'd help protect me."

Mother exhaled a sigh that was part terror, part relief. "You could have been arrested if you'd been caught stealing correspondence. Did you know that?" Henry fussed weakly in her arms, and she rocked him.

"But, Mother, these are the plans to attack Whitemarsh! Father's regiment! And it will be a surprise attack!" I said.

"Yes, I see that," Mother said. "We must warn them. We'll have to get this dispatch to General Washington."

She handed Henry to me. I could feel the heat of the baby's fever through his wrapping. His little face was dry and red, and his lips were cracked.

Mother went to the window and stood there, looking out at the snowy farmyard. "What shall we do? I must think." She paused. "The dispatch must be carried in person. The officers at Whitemarsh will not trust spoken information. I will have to leave immediately."

"Whitemarsh is thirteen miles away," I said. "Too far to walk."

"I'll take Brownie." Mother turned around, twisting her hands. "The roads are very risky. Redcoat sentries are everywhere, and they are on a constant lookout for Patriot spies. Should I not return by tomorrow at noon—"

"Should you not return!" I burst out. "Mother, no! You cannot leave us—you cannot leave Henry. He's too sick." I took a deep breath as an idea began to form in my mind, gathering strength like a growing storm. "Let me go."

My words fell like clinking pennies into the suddenly silent room. Benjamin and Mother both gaped at me.

"You go?" Mother said. "No! No, Rebecca, it's far too dangerous."

"Mother, please!" I exclaimed. Henry fussed, and I realized I was squeezing him by accident. I handed him back to Mother. "Don't you see? It's the only way!"

"Rebecca, no." Mother shook her head. "A young girl, out on her own . . ."

I thought rapidly. "Don't you see? That's exactly why it *will* work. No one will suspect me—a girl—of carrying information. I'll say

I'm searching for a doctor for Henry. They'll wave me through the checkpoints."

I could see realization dawning slowly and reluctantly on Mother's face. "We will have to conceal the dispatch very well . . . ," she said.

"Then you give your permission?" I asked. I held my breath.

"Yes, I suppose," Mother said slowly.

I clasped my hands. A secret thrill of excitement and fear shot through me. I was riding to Whitemarsh!

"We must work quickly," Mother said. She seemed energized now that we had a plan.

She placed Henry in his cradle and stirred up the fire until it burst into leaping flames. "Benjamin, bring me my sewing box. Rebecca, get your cloak. I'll make up some cornbread for you to take, but first we have to conceal the dispatch."

"How?" I asked. I grabbed my red woolen cloak from where it hung on its peg by the door and handed it to her.

"Watch," Mother said.

Working carefully, she loosened the fabric covering the big button that fastened the cloak together. I had made the button myself from a piece of wood. Normally, the fabric was drawn tightly over the button and sewn into a bunch underneath.

As I watched, Mother carefully picked out the stitches that fastended the fabric to the underside of the button.

"Now give me the dispatch," she said, holding out her hand.

I handed it to her. Mother folded the paper into a small, smooth square. She placed the square over the bare wood of the button. Then she stretched the fabric back over the button,

hiding the dispatch, and sewed it back into a bunch underneath.

"There!" Mother said, holding up the cloak.

"You can't see the dispatch at all!" I said, taking it in my own hand and admiring it. "No one will look for it there."

"Yes," Mother said. "That's better than a message hidden at the bottom of a saddlebag or rolled into a needle book. I have heard of messages being hidden in those places—and then found by the sentries."

I shivered suddenly at the thought of rough hands dragging out the contents of my saddlebag, the shouting when they found the message, then—

"The fire's hot, Mother," Benjamin said, interrupting my thoughts.

"Mix up the cornbread, Rebecca," Mother directed. "Benjamin, gather your sister's warmest stockings and get my big shawl from the trunk."

Henry started crying again, and Mother picked him up and rocked him. "Oh, he is so very hot. Benjamin, don't stand there—hurry!"

The rest of the evening passed in a bustle of packing cornbread, picking up clothes and putting them down, and warnings from Mother about the danger of the road.

"You must be as innocent and sweet as you can, daughter," she said before bed, quickly sewing up a hole in my stockings before the last light of the dying fire. "The sentries have been fooled by people posing as messengers before, so they will be on high alert."

"They won't suspect me," I said, trying to convince both of us.

"They will suspect a girl less, this is true," Mother agreed, "but it does not mean you are not under suspicion! Be as simple as you can. Say only that you are searching for a doctor."

"I will." I tried to sound braver than I felt. The house was so cozy with the lamplight and the fire, and my toes were so warm. Mother and Benjamin and Henry were there. I didn't want to leave this place and go out into the cold, snowy world.

But I didn't have a choice. My father's life depended on me.

Philadelphia, Pennsylvania
December 3, 1777
6:00 a.m.

The next morning, I woke early. The pale sun was just sending pink and gold rays over the snow. It didn't seem real, what I was about to do. Not until I sat on Brownie, in front of the cabin, with Mother and Benjamin looking up at me.

From inside the cabin, I could hear Henry's weak wailing. He had cried all night—until he had no strength left—but yet he was still crying.

I wondered if he would live to see my return, then pushed that thought away.

He will, I told myself. *Of course he will. Mother won't let him die.*

I looked down at her. She was biting her bottom lip, the way she always did when she was trying not to cry.

"Brownie will take care of me, Mother," I said. The horse's big, warm body under mine was a comfort, especially with the thin morning air whipping my cheeks.

"Yes, he is your partner now," Mother said. She patted my boot, trying to smile up at me. Her eyes glittered with unshed tears. "Ride hard and do not allow yourself to be captured. Nothing would be worse than that."

I could think of something worse, but I didn't say. Benjamin looked up at me. I knew he was thinking it too.

"Good luck, Becky," he said. He hadn't called me that since he was little.

"Goodbye, Benji." I leaned down awkwardly and gave him a quick hug. "Take care of Mother," I whispered. He nodded.

A lump was growing in my throat. I wanted to fling myself off Brownie and run back into the safe, warm house. But then I touched the precious message hidden under my button. I thought of Father, his bare feet bound up with rags, huddled around his fire in the snow.

I picked up the reins. "Walk, Brownie," I ordered.

The horse started out of the barnyard. I looked back only once. Mother and Benjamin stood there, pressed together, waving.

With a wave of my own, I guided Brownie out the familiar gate, onto the road—and into the unknown.

CHAPTER FIVE

Brownie's hooves clopped on the frozen, rutted road. At first, women with baskets and men riding horses passed by, nodding at me. A wagon trundled past, loaded with firewood.

On the other side of the road, clapboard houses were clustered together, their chimneys pouring smoke from the morning fires. I could smell pork frying and inhaled as if it were perfume.

Brownie walked calmly, chewing his bit and occasionally tossing his head with a jingle of his bridle. His familiar gait soothed me as the houses thinned on either side. Fields stretched out, dotted with stubble from the harvested corn stalks. Everything was coated with blown snow.

Soon there were no more passersby—the houses were behind me now, and no one was in the fields at this time of year.

Brownie's sides were warm against my stockinged legs, but my hands quickly grew numb on the reins. I changed my grip frequently, tucking my free hand under my cloak. My face felt stiff, and my toes were already like wooden blocks.

Still, I kept going. I passed four of the stone markers. That was four miles—almost one third of the way. One third of the way to Father.

I sang to the horse to break the silence and the tedium. *"'Twas summer, and softly the breezes were blowing, and sweetly the nightingale sang from the tree. At the foot of a hill, where the river was flowing, I sat myself down on the banks of the Dee."*

Brownie flicked one ear back at the sound of my voice. I thought of him as a colt, when he would race up to me in the pasture. He would pretend to butt me with his head, as if I were another colt too.

"Don't let him play with you as if you were his equal," Father had said when he saw this game. "He'll not respect you if he thinks he can lead you."

Every day after that, Father had gone to the pasture with me. He had shown me how to stand quietly, not rewarding Brownie's antics, until the horse calmed down and came to me for the apple and the halter I held.

My throat swelled and ached at the memory. *Father, I'm coming!* I called in my mind.

Just then, a square building became visible in front of me. Gradually, it grew larger and larger. Eventually I could see that it was a well-built, two-story house. A hitching post and sign swinging on hinges stood out front.

I was too far yet to make out the words, but I could see men gathered around the entrance. They stood in groups, smoke rising up from their pipes.

My hands grew sweaty. *This must be the Blue Boar Tavern,* I realized.

Father had mentioned it once or twice. He said it was no place for girls. It sat at the crossroads between the road to Whitemarsh and the road to Germantown. I would have to pass it now and face all those eyes.

Will they question me? I wondered. *A young girl, out alone?*

Brownie seemed to sense the tension in my body too. He walked more quickly, pricking his ears at the movement and smells ahead, then flicking one ear back toward me.

The tavern was growing closer now. I could make out the lettering on the sign. BLUE BOAR it said, as I had thought. The men were closer now too. I could smell their pipe smoke and hear the faint rumble of their voices.

Are they Patriots or Loyalists? I wondered. They were clad in ordinary clothes, not uniforms, so there was no way to tell.

I fixed my eyes straight ahead and steadied my hand on Brownie's reins. "We don't have to talk to them," I said quietly, as much to the horse as to myself. "We have just as much right to be on this road as they do."

The men turned to look as I approached. The door to the tavern was open, and I could hear voices inside and clanking dishes.

"Hey now!" a rough voice called. "A girl alone! What's your business then, young lady?" It was a youngish man with red hair spilling onto the shoulders of his jacket. He held a long pipe in one hand and a metal tankard in the other.

Laughter followed from the others, and I gritted my teeth. My hand was slippery with sweat but I knew I mustn't let them see.

"Get down, rest a spell!" another called out.

Brownie and I were passing right by them now. Brownie tossed his head but, good horse that he was, did not vary his stride.

"Nay then, John Smith!" a woman's voice called. A maid had come to the door, a comfortable woman with a stained apron wrapped around her middle. She held a mug in one hand and a dishcloth in the other. "Leave that girl in peace!"

The men roared with laughter, and I squeezed my heels into Brownie's sides so he picked up a trot. I could feel the men's eyes burning into my back. It wasn't until the tavern was safely in the distance that I finally let out a sigh.

"We did it, Brownie," I murmured.

I relaxed and let my feet dangle out of the stirrups. We kept marching down the road, Brownie stepping briskly, his head bobbing. I closed my eyes for a moment, dozing.

When I opened them, I saw nothing but snowy fields, stands of trees, and gray sky. My hands were growing numb, and I kept switching them off the reins, tucking one under my cloak.

Suddenly I sat up straight in the saddle. My heart gave a great thud in my chest. Up ahead, a Redcoat was standing to the side of the road. A sentry—my first checkpoint.

This man wouldn't be sloppy like the men at the tavern. He would be alert and on the lookout for anyone suspicious. I could see him clearly now, his musket at his side, his red wool coat crisscrossed with soiled straps of white canvas.

Innocent and young, I reminded myself.

That was how Mother said I must behave. Simply a girl out looking for a doctor for her sick brother—nothing more, nothing less.

"Halt!" the sentry cried, spotting me. I drew rein on Brownie so hard he reared back slightly. "What is your business?"

The man's face was unshaven, and his beady eyes went over me from head to toe. The button with the message seemed to be burning a hole right through my dress and into my skin.

Can he see the wrinkles in the fabric? I worried. I wanted to touch it but forced my hands to stay quiet on the reins.

"Sir, I am seeking a doctor for my little brother. He is very sick." My voice came out high and tight. Beneath my cloak, my heart was hammering like Brownie running in the fields.

The man narrowed his eyes. "A doctor? What are you doing looking for a doctor out here?"

He swept his hand at the empty fields around them. "You'd be better off asking at the Blue Boar. That's four miles back. Didn't you think to ask there?"

I thought fast. "Oh-oh, I did! Ask there. The maid said the doctor was . . . headed this way. To deliver a baby at one of the farms." I swallowed and tried an innocent smile.

He didn't smile back. "I would have seen the doctor. This is the only road north. No one has passed. Dismount," he ordered. "Empty your saddlebags."

I just stared at him, my mouth dry. What had I done?

CHAPTER SIX

He suspected! In a cloud of fear, I slid off Brownie's back. I fumbled at my saddlebag strings with numb fingers. The package of cornbread fell to the snowy ground, and the string came loose. The sentry and I both stared at the cornbread, lying on the churned-up snow.

"What else?" he demanded. He plunged his hand into the leather bags. Brownie shied at the touch of this smelly stranger.

"I have nothing else." My voice was audibly shaking. "Please, sir, let me pass."

For a moment that seemed to stretch into eternity, the sentry paused. Then, finally, he nodded.

I'm free!

Without waiting for him to change his mind, I scooped the wet package of cornbread from the snow and shoved it into the saddlebag again. With difficulty, I mounted Brownie from the ground, then kicked him up into a canter.

I knew the faster pace meant risking a fall on the slippery road, but I had to put some distance between us and the sentry. A mile up, I drew rein and breathed deeply. I guessed I was about halfway to Whitemarsh.

"I'm coming, Father!" I called out. Brownie sensed the change in energy and pranced against the tight rein. He was ready to go too.

The snow was not as slick here, and the footing was safer. I loosened the rein and leaned forward.

Brownie took off, tossing his head so that his bridle jingled. I let him stretch out and enjoy the run, my body rocking with his stride.

The wind was cold against my sweaty face, and my cloak billowed out behind me. *At this rate, I'll make Whitemarsh before sunset,* I thought.

I imagined Father's face when I handed him the message. He'd grab me up in a hug, and I'd sit close beside him at the fire, telling him all the news from home. Together, we'd give the dispatch to General Washington's assistant.

I was coming up on a forest ahead. The road narrowed here, and roots poked out of the dirty snow.

"Whoa, whoa." I slowed Brownie to a trot and posted while we both caught our breath.

Suddenly voices came from ahead. I halted Brownie and listened. A group of people was

coming through the woods from the other side—
men. I could hear the jingle of boots and spurs and
see flashes of red.

Redcoats, I realized. I had to hide.

"Brownie, here, here," I whispered, urging the
horse into the trees. If I could just get far enough
back and hold still, perhaps they would pass without
seeing. "Please, come on!"

I kicked at my horse, but he balked at walking
farther into the dark, crowded woods. The men were
getting closer.

". . . twelve miles and the lieutenant kept them
marching," one was saying. "No time to make
camp."

"The Patriot devils must have been on their
tails," another replied.

Brownie planted his feet and tossed his head
against my urging. There must have been some
smell, something back in the woods he didn't like.

"Please!" I begged.

I twirled the reins and caught Brownie on one shoulder, then the other, trying to force him forward. But the horse threw his head up and rolled his eyes dangerously.

"You there!" a rough voice called.

Too late. They had spotted me.

"Stop!" another one said.

In a moment, they surrounded me. There were six or seven men, all pressing in close. I could smell their unwashed bodies. The scent hovered like a cloud around them. They wore scraggly beards, and greasy hair poked from under their caps.

Brownie reared back, trying to get away from the men and their unfamiliar scent. I gripped the reins, trying not to panic.

"A girl!" one of the men said. His teeth showed brown in his beard. "And all alone."

"This is what we find out on patrol, is it?" another one said.

I could tell he was a sergeant. His hat had a feather in it, and his red wool sash had a symbol sewn in the center. I'd seen it many times while delivering vegetables. The others must be privates. Their tall, buff-colored hats had no feathers.

"Here we were searching for something to eat," he continued, "and all we find is this one sorry specimen."

"We could eat *her!*" another man said. They all burst into laughter, crowding around while fear twisted my stomach.

"Please! Let me pass." My voice was small. "I'm searching for a doctor for my little brother."

The sergeant regarded me carefully. He had bright blue eyes that seemed to look right into my head. "Searching for a doctor, are you? All alone out here?"

The others grew quiet. I nodded, hardly daring to breath. Trickles of sweat ran down the sides of my face.

"I've been hearing reports in camp of female spies in this area," the sergeant said. "Women alone, pretending to be sweet and innocent."

My breath caught. *He suspected! He suspected!* my mind screamed.

My legs clamped involuntarily on Brownie's sides. The horse, thinking it was a command to go, leaped forward.

"Stop her!" the sergeant shouted.

A private jumped ahead and grabbed hold of Brownie's reins. The horse squealed and plunged, spinning in his tracks. I lost a stirrup and barely managed to keep my seat, grabbing the saddle to steady myself. The private hung onto the reins, dragging at Brownie's mouth.

"Please, let me go!" I cried.

"We'll take her back to camp," the sergeant said to his men. "We can decide what to do with her there." He looked up at me with those odd blue eyes. "And if we find out you are a spy, little girl, your brother is going to be the least of your worries."

CHAPTER SEVEN

Pennsylvania countryside
December 3, 1777
4:00 p.m.

The men led us back the way I'd come, out through the woods and into another little gathering of trees. The soldiers surrounded me on all sides, laughing and talking as they walked. One led Brownie, and the sergeant himself walked at my stirrup, where he could see my every move.

I clung to the saddle, my stomach rolling with worry, my mind spinning. The worst had happened—I'd been captured. And they suspected me of being a spy. All they would have to do now is find the dispatch.

I had to do something. I could try kicking Brownie so that he bolted ahead, but without reins, I would surely fall. They'd be upon me in an instant.

Should I try signaling to some sympathetic person passing on the road? I thought.

I quickly dismissed the idea. There was no way to know who was a Loyalist and who a Patriot. And there was no one around, especially now, as the soldiers led me deeper into the snow-covered trees.

"Please, where are you taking me?" I ventured to ask after what seemed like a long time.

"Camp," the sergeant said shortly. He offered no more explanation.

After a few more minutes, we came to a clearing where a few large boulders offered a natural shelter. I could see signs of a camp about: a dead fire ringed with stones, a few pots laying nearby, trampled, dirty snow. Three horses stood tied to low tree branches on the other side of the clearing.

"Dismount," the sergeant ordered.

I slid off clumsily, nearly falling in the snow, and stood there shivering. I clutched the cloak with its precious button around me, not daring to look at the soldiers' faces, lest they should read my secret.

The men stood in a ring around me. "What are we going to do with her, Sergeant?" one of them asked.

The sergeant stared at me for a long moment. "That is what we have to decide," he said. He motioned to the dead fire. "Go warm yourself."

One of the other soldiers, a skinny one who looked no older than a boy, knelt down beside the ashes. He quickly kindled a blaze with a flint and steel. I held out my purple hands, keeping my eyes fixed on the soldiers and Brownie every second.

The men stood in a group, talking, and then one of them led Brownie to the other horses.

He tied the reins up to the saddle, then tied Brownie to a low tree branch using a length of rope.

"I say take her to the main camp now," one of the soldiers said. "If she's not a spy, she's a Patriot and up to something. They'll detain her there."

My breath quickened. *Detain me!*

Then the sergeant spoke: "We've no officers here. You men know we can't proceed without an officer's orders." He turned to the young private. "Cook, you'll go. Take a horse and ride out to the encampment. Tell Captain Miller we've found a suspected spy. It'll take you most of the night. We'll wait for you here."

Cook nodded. A few minutes later, he pounded out of the camp on a black pony.

I stared at the leaping orange flames. I was trapped. We were hostages, Brownie and I, and the clock was ticking! The sun was already low in the sky, and the attack was to be tomorrow at dawn.

I have to get to Whitemarsh, I thought frantically. *I have to warn Father.*

I wrapped my arms around my middle and leaned over, trying to contain the sickening mixture of fear and anxiety rolling around inside me.

If I did nothing, Cook would fetch the officer. They'd question me and find the dispatch and take me to their prison. General Howe would attack Whitemarsh, and Father and his soldiers would be caught without their weapons in their hands. They'd be slaughtered, and Mother would be alone with only Benjamin to help her.

A sob escaped me, and I leaned my head on my knees. A moment later, a pair of legs approached and stood in front of me. I looked up. The sergeant stood over me, hands on his hips.

"Out looking for a doctor?" he asked. "That's what you said?"

I didn't dare look at him. I nodded at the ground.

"Take your hood down," he said roughly.

I stood and tried to untie the strings of my hood. The other soldiers were watching silently. My fingers were shaking badly from nerves and cold. Finally I fumbled it free and stood with my eyes cast down.

The sergeant gave me a hard stare. "Shoes," he ordered.

I hesitated. I'd never taken my shoes off out of the house before. It seemed inappropriate.

"Shoes!" the sergeant shouted.

I had no choice. I scrambled to undo the buckles and stood in front of the men, the snow soaking into my woolen stockings as they looked inside my shoes. I clutched my cloak around me. The secret button seemed to stand out like a beacon, declaring its secret to everyone.

"Now your cloak," the sergeant said.

Can they sense my hesitation? I worried.

I wrapped my fingers around the button as I undid it, asking it to stay quiet. Silently, I unwrapped the cloak.

I stood with my eyes fixed ahead, my heart hammering so hard I thought surely the men would see it through my dress. The cold pierced my clothes as the sergeant held the cloak up by the hood. He examined the seams and pockets.

Not the button! He ignored the button! I could hardly believe it. Mother's disguise had worked.

The sergeant handed back my cloak and shoes. I quickly put them back on, trying to arrange my face in calm lines.

Realizing there was nothing to see, the privates turned away from me. They unpacked their knapsacks and kindled a second campfire, scooping tea into a battered metal kettle.

"You'll sit here." The sergeant pointed at a spot on the ground near the first campfire. A rough, gray woolen blanket landed at my feet. "Keep warm with this," he ordered.

I nodded without looking up. It wasn't until the sergeant had moved away to the other side of the campsite that I allowed myself a small measure of relief. I needed to sit and think.

I crouched over the spluttering flames of my fire and tried to take stock. These things I knew for certain: One, I was trapped. Two, in the morning, the officer would be here to take charge of me. Three, by then, the attack would have happened.

I can't let that happen, I thought.

The shadows were gathering under the trees now, and the sun was sending its last rays through the branches. Soon, twilight made the shapes blurry.

The soldiers must have had something more than coffee in their knapsacks because I saw a jug passing from hand to hand, lit by their campfire.

The talking grew louder, broken occasionally by snatches of singing. No one seemed to be paying attention to me now. Perhaps they thought one girl on her own would never dare to try to escape.

Well, they thought wrong, I told myself.

It didn't matter if the officer they'd gone to fetch thought I was a spy or not. If I didn't escape tonight, my whole mission would be for nothing.

But how? When the soldiers saw me gone, they'd catch me in an instant. I had a basic sense of the road—straight through those trees—but the soldiers would know that also.

I must have a horse, I realized. I was a strong rider. On horseback, I'd gain precious minutes. The soldiers could ride too, but they were heavier—and possibly drunk now. I was willing to bet I could outrun them.

Keeping an eye on the second campfire, I scooted quietly back a few feet. I craned my neck to see

Brownie and the other horses tethered to the branch. They were just big shapes in the darkness, only visible against the glowing snow, but I could see that Brownie stood a little apart from the others. Something about the way he was standing looked different.

Then it hit me—a rope was hanging straight down from his halter. He'd untied his tether!

Of course! I wanted to shout out loud. Brownie always untied any rope that didn't have a clove hitch. I had known that since I was six. But of course, the soldiers didn't.

If I could just reach him, I could gallop out of the campsite. Perhaps I'd even get a few moments' head start before the men came after me.

It would be risky and dangerous, but it was worth it. I had a message to deliver.

CHAPTER EIGHT

Pennsylvania countryside
December 3, 1777
7:00 p.m.

I waited and watched. A sliver of moon rose in the eastern sky. My campfire burned low, but the soldiers did not come to build it up again. They were drawn up around their own fire, the leaping flames lighting up their faces. They talked loudly among one another, passing their jug from hand to hand, sometimes breaking into song.

Across the camp the logs crackled, sending an occasional shower of sparks into the black sky. The men seemed to have forgotten about me entirely.

I gathered all my courage. Moving slowly, I scooted backward, away from my campfire, outside the ring of light. I paused. No one seemed to have noticed my movements.

My breath coming quickly now, I gathered my cloak and its precious button around me. I crawled toward the edge of the campsite.

If I could just make it to the shelter of the trees, I could slip through to the horses. I only prayed none of them would sense my movement and whinny, giving me away.

The wetness of the snow bit through my stockings. I didn't dare look up in case I should see the soldiers standing over me. I was halfway to the trees before I hazarded a glance over my shoulder. They hadn't moved.

"And now again, lads," the sergeant was shouting, the unmistakable slur of drink in his voice. *"When we were home again, dear . . ."*

As the others soldiers joined in, something bumped against my hand. I felt it over quickly— damp canvas, leather, and buckles—it was one of their packs.

An idea flashed into my head. *What if . . .*
I could make my escape easier?

With numb, shaking fingers, I quickly undid one of the buckles and plunged my hand inside. I felt past a lumpy package, bits of leather, and a bridle bit. Finally, I felt something hard—the brim of a cap.

I pulled it out and dug deeper into the pack, unearthing a roll of clothing. Hurriedly, with my eyes fixed on the campfire, I shook it out. White breeches, like the ones the soldiers were wearing.

My heart pounding, I fumbled the pants on under my dress and stuffed the skirt down the waistband. Then I bundled my braids on top of my head and pulled the cap down over them.

"Stop!" the sergeant suddenly said from his place by the fire. He held up his hand, and I froze, my blood turning to ice water. "How is it we've passed half the night and not sung 'The Blasted Herb'?"

The other men cheered loudly, and I breathed again. But I could not delay one instant more. All they had to do was walk across to my fire and they'd see I was gone.

I crawled to the safety of the trees—fast. Once the trunks surrounded me, I got to my feet and ran, stumbling over the snow, to the tree where the horses were tied up. I prayed they would not whinny and give me away.

Please be silent, I begged Brownie in my head. He was dozing with his hind foot cocked. The rope hung freely from his halter.

It was now or never. Once I moved, I would have only an instant before the soldiers saw me.

I took two deep breaths and summoned Father's face before my eyes for strength. Then I slipped out from behind the tree and grasped Brownie's rope, flipping it up onto his neck.

In that moment, I realized a horrible fact— Brownie was not wearing his bridle. It was slung over the saddle horn. He wore only his halter and the rope.

I had no time to think, though. I could only scramble up onto his back with one foot in the stirrup. The other horses, startled by my movements, jerked back on their ropes and began to plunge about with alarm.

"The horses!" I heard one of the men shout.

I gathered the rope in my hands—as close to reins as I was going to get—crouched low over Brownie's neck, and hammered my heels into his sides. Instantly he sprang back and away from the tree, almost unseating me.

For a terrifying instant, I slid dangerously to one side of the saddle. Then I managed to balance, yanking Brownie's face around using the rope and halter, and kicked him as hard as I could.

"Go, go!" I cried.

Brownie leaped into a gallop with a huge heave, clearly as scared as I was. He ran directly through the soldiers's campfire before any of them could realize what was going on. Soot, snow, and burning logs spun away from his legs, and the soldiers dived for safety to either side.

Behind me, I could hear the other horses rearing up. One, a big, white gelding, snapped his rope and ran through the camp after us, his eyes rolling.

"The bay! The bay! With a boy!" someone called.

I didn't dare look back. I knew it wasn't a boy they were talking about. It was me.

CHAPTER NINE

Brownie galloped madly. I could only pray he wouldn't collide with a tree. Finally the trees thinned, and through my half-open eyes, I could see the white of the snowy road ahead.

Brownie burst through the trees, sliding on the packed snow of the road. I tried to rein him in—he must not slip and fall on the ice. He ignored me, though, and plunged on down the road, galloping for all he was worth.

I clung to the rope and his mane, casting a fevered glance over my shoulder. Two mounted

horsemen had just appeared through the trees too.
I could see the shapes of their horses and their white
breeches in the faint starlight.

Without thinking, I yanked Brownie's face
to the left so sharply he half slid down a small
embankment. A dense clump of shrubs sat at the
bottom, and I urged him behind the shield.

Above me, the two Redcoats pounded past,
hoping to overtake me on the road, no doubt. I tried
to control my ragged breathing as they passed.
Thankfully no one else followed on foot—the others
must have stayed at camp.

I forced myself to wait until long after the
horsemen had disappeared. Then I dismounted and
slipped Brownie's bridle over his head.

Urging the horse back up onto the road, I caught
my breath and wiped my cloak over my sweaty face.
The crescent moon was climbing overhead. I judged
it must be near midnight. I must hurry.

Whitemarsh lay west of the Great Bog. The vast tract of land was wild, marshy, and full of strange plants and birds. I knew I must not stumble into the treacherous, peaty ground.

If I did, Brownie and I could be trapped in the quicksand that dotted the bog. A boy and his horse had died there last year.

The Redcoats would be looking for me on the main road. But I was willing to bet they didn't know about the path that skirted the edge of the bog. A rider could splash through the river at a low place and find him or herself right at the edge of the vast meadow where General Washington's army was encamped.

I remembered playing in Whitemarsh's vast meadow in the summertime, the river bordering one edge. I had looked across to the Great Bog and its strange, uneven ground. Now I would be approaching from the opposite direction.

I urged Brownie on with whispers. He plodded ahead, tired now, his head drooping. Finally the great, empty expanse of the bog spread out before us. At the edge, the bushes stopped.

During the day, I would have been able to see the snow-coated grasses, but in the dark, I could only see what looked like a white sea of snow. It spread out, glowing before me.

A faint path worn by deer ran along the edge of the bushes. Carefully, I guided Brownie to it, being sure he stepped only where I could see deer tracks. If the ground could support the deer, it could support us.

On and on I rode, with only the occasional hoot of an owl to break the silent winter night. I grew sleepy in the saddle and occasionally dozed.

In my mind, I saw Father, grinning as he came up the path to the house on a summer day. Benjamin and I jumped in the haystack behind the house, the sun warm above us. Brownie bobbed his head at the pasture gate, waiting for his apple, and then he halted, and suddenly I was awake.

We had arrived at the river.

It flowed like black ink, cutting a path through the snowy banks. Boulders topped with snow sat scattered through the water.

The water was deeper than I remembered from the summer—and very different from the sparkling, burbling stream that had rushed under the hot sun. I knew how slick the icy stones would be . . . how slippery the footing. Every inch of my skin recoiled at the thought of crossing.

I stood in the stirrups and strained my eyes across the river. I could just make out the orange lights of the campfires—the army was over there. Father was over there. I had to try.

Bracing myself, I squeezed Brownie forward. He picked his way hesitantly up to the riverbank, then paused, his ears pricked as he regarded the rushing water.

"Go, boy! Go!" I urged him.

Brownie trusted me. I could sense that, at least. Delicately, he splashed into the black river. I gasped as the water splashed up to my stirrups. I'd thought the snow and ice and wind were the coldest things on earth. And now I saw I was wrong.

The water was growing deeper. Brownie was picking his way carefully, trying not to lose his balance against the slick, rounded stones. I gave him his head and tried not to get in his way.

We were halfway across now, and the water was up to Brownie's knees. My feet were soaked. Pins of icy numbness stabbed them. If the water grew any deeper, I didn't know if Brownie would keep his balance. He'd be swept downriver and me with him. My message would be lost, along with my life.

I held the wet reins, clinging to Brownie's wet mane, and prayed. It must have been heard because the water grew more shallow. The bank was closer now.

Brownie sensed it too and stepped briskly and more confidently. With a final splash and a scramble up the bank, we were out—and safely on the other side.

I rested for a minute, letting Brownie rest as well. I touched numb fingers to the precious button, reassuring myself it was still there. Then, I tried to squeeze Brownie forward, only to find my feet frozen to the stirrups.

With difficulty, I pulled them loose, hearing the ice crackle. The tired horse plodded forward.

The campfire lights were larger now that we were across the river. I could see dark figures moving in front of them. I strained my eyes, trying to see if I could spot Father's shadow.

"Halt!" a rough voice shouted. "Who's there?"

The guards, I realized. *Of course.*

I flung my hood back from my face as two figures appeared in the dark. One of them held up a lantern.

"Please, sirs, I am Rebecca Williams," I said, teeth chattering. "I come with an important message for General Washington. My father is Colin Williams. He is encamped here with his regiment."

My voice sounded thin and wavery, even to my ears. I wished I didn't feel so weak. I wished I could feel my legs.

"A girl!" one of the guards said. "This is no place for you! Get away! Get back to your home, girl!" He and the other guard turned away, taking the light of the lantern and the last of my strength with them.

"No!" I suddenly screamed. My voice broke. "No, I won't! I have a message about General

Howe's assault! He will attack you at dawn, do you see? He will slaughter you all and my father too and there is sickness at our house, Mother cannot last, so let me through, let me through—"

"Hysterical!" one of the men said.

"And frozen to the bone," the other agreed.

Fury surged through me. I'd ridden miles in the snow, been captured, escaped, and forded the frozen creek. I hadn't come this far only to be dismissed as a silly girl.

I looked down into the soldiers' faces, then kicked Brownie into a trot, riding right past them and into the camp.

"Stop!" one of them shouted.

I ignored them. I wasn't going to stop—not now.

CHAPTER **TEN**

"Who is this?" someone else said as I rode farther into camp.

"A girl, sir," one of the guards answered. "She claims she has a message for the general, but how should we believe her?"

I steadied myself and spoke loudly and clearly. "My father is Colin Williams. He is part of the Philadelphia County Militia. I have come into important information regarding an attack on this camp by General Howe. Please direct me to my father, so that I may pass him the message."

I stopped, exhausted by my efforts.

My clear words had had an effect on the soldiers now crowding around me. They muttered to one another and then one, an officer, stepped aside and nodded.

"Dismount, miss," he said. "We'll rub down and water your horse. He looks done in. Corporal Williams is over here."

I slid off Brownie and patted his damp, hot neck. "Good boy," I whispered, pressing my face close to his fur. "You've saved the regiment."

A solider took the reins and led Brownie away. The horse went eagerly, perhaps sensing that a bucket of oats and a warm blanket awaited him after our long journey.

My knees shook with exhaustion now that I was standing. My feet were like frozen blocks of wood. I stumbled suddenly, and the officer caught my arm.

"This way," he said. "Williams is with his troop over here."

My heart beat fast under my cloak as I fought the pain in my feet. I strained to catch Father's figure in the shadows that seemed to be everywhere.

Then suddenly, somehow, he was before me, his face obscured by a bushy, reddish beard. But it was him—my own dear father—opening his arms and folding me to his chest.

"My dear daughter!" he said.

"Father!" I sobbed into his chest. "I've brought such important news!" Looking up, I saw tears glistening in the wrinkles at the corners of his eyes.

"You're so cold, little daughter." Father led me beside a nearby fire and spread a blanket over a log, drawing it up close to the leaping flames. He wrapped a second blanket over my shoulders. From another solider, he accepted a steaming tin mug and handed it to me. "Drink this."

I sipped at the scalding tea. As warmth began spreading through me, I spoke. "Father, a message—I've come carrying an important message."

I explained how I'd come by the dispatch as a growing circle of soldiers listened in silence.

"And it's here, in my cloak button!" I finished. I struggled to unfasten it, but my numb fingers would not cooperate.

"Here, daughter, let me," Father said. Tenderly, he unfastened the cloak, draping his own wool jacket around my shoulders as protection against the cold.

"It's under the cloth," I said. "Be careful!"

Every eye was on Father as he carefully slit the fabric with his knife. The edge of the folded paper appeared, and everyone exhaled. Father drew it out through the opening. He unfolded the paper and read it silently, then stood up.

"Get this to General Washington immediately," he said to a young solider standing beside him. "Howe is planning a surprise attack by dawn!"

The soldiers around us scattered to begin preparations. Around the camp, the call spread: "Howe will attack! Ready the guns! To arms! Get the powder ready!"

Horses were being led from place to place. I could hear the clink of muskets and buckles. I knew I would feel glad later, but right now, all I felt was a bone-weary exhaustion.

Father knelt beside me and took my face in his hands. "You have saved the regiment. Because of your journey, we have time to prepare for the attack. And we will be ready."

"Just come home safe, Father," I whispered. "That's all I want."

Father kissed me on the forehead. "And that's what you'll have. But first we must win this battle."

Henry was better. I could see that the moment I came down the ladder from the sleeping loft. His awful flush was gone, and he slept peacefully in his cradle by the fire while Mother cut up apples at the table.

"Have you slept enough, finally?" Mother asked, laughing up at me.

"Is it morning?" I looked at the sunlight streaming through the windowpanes. I rubbed my eyes and looked again.

Mother nodded. "When you came in at dawn yesterday you were so cold and weary you could hardly stagger through the door. You slept all day and all night. But here, I have your stockings waiting for you, all dry and clean."

I dropped into a chair and pulled on the warm stockings, trying to clear my head. I barely remembered the ride home, only that Brownie and I had been so tired we could barely stand.

I had a vague memory of sliding off Brownie in the yard and Mother helping me into the house when my legs wouldn't hold me anymore. But after that, nothing.

Then it hit me. The battle!

I sat up in my chair. "Mother! Is there news of the battle? Father?"

Mother shook her head. "Nothing yet. But Matthew Dobson was wounded at the battle and has come home. Benjamin is at his house, waiting to hear the news."

Just then, the door banged open. Benjamin stood there, the cold air pouring in around him.

"Skirmishes! Nothing more!" he gasped. "Howe attacked, but our men were ready. They fought

so well that Howe called off the assault! He's
retreating as we speak!"

I gave a whoop of joy, and Mother clasped
me to her chest. "You did it, my dear!" She held
my face in her hands and kissed me. "We are so
proud."

I was filled with joy. My ride had not been for
nothing. The men had had time to prepare. Father
was safe—the others were too. For now, he would
march on through the cold and snow with General
Washington to Valley Forge. But one day, he would
come home to us. And in the meantime, somehow,
we would survive. I would make sure of that.

A NOTE FROM THE AUTHOR

I live in an old part of Cincinnati, Ohio—in a suburb called Wyoming—about six hundred miles from Philadelphia, Pennsylvania, where Rebecca's story takes place.

Six hundred miles is a long way. Much of the American Revolution was fought in what are now the states of Pennsylvania, Massachusetts, New Jersey, New York, and South Carolina, not in Ohio. But although the fighting was far away, Cincinnati still holds remnants of Rebecca's time—the period surrounding the American Revolution.

Route 4 is one such remnant. It's been a road—or at least a path—since the mid-eighteenth century. This busy, four-lane road starts at the banks of the Ohio River and runs north through the city, right past my house. It continues past the grocery store and the big Goodwill and the nature preserve.

At one point, Route 4 forks. At the fork sits a tavern called the Century Inn.

Today, the Century Inn has sand volleyball and neon signs. But on a plaque out front, the Century Inn reminds us that it opened its doors in 1801—in Rebecca's lifetime. Back then, fields and wild woods stretched on either side. Now there's a condo complex with a man-made pond.

When I wrote about the Blue Boar, the tavern Rebecca passes on her brave journey, I saw the Century Inn in my mind. So many questions crossed my mind: What might it have looked like when Rebecca was alive? Did the barkeep come to the door with a rag in his hand to look out onto the frozen dirt road? Did riders and carriages pull up at all hours of the day, glad for a warm fire and a mug of ale after their long ride from the river?

Route 4 and the Century Inn weren't my only inspirations. While the story of Rebecca is fictional,

I drew on the true stories of many brave women and girls who helped the Patriots during the American Revolution.

The lives of three women in particular captured my imagination: Sybil Ludington, Lydia Darragh, and Deborah Champion.

Like Rebecca, Sybil and Deborah made nighttime horseback rides with important messages for Patriot leadership. Both Sybil and Deborah were teenagers when they mounted their horses and galloped through the countryside. Deborah made her journey disguised as an old woman.

Lydia Darragh was a wife and mother when she overheard British officers billeted in her house discussing secret plans to attack Whitemarsh—a real place just north of Philadelphia. Lydia walked many miles in the snow, leaving her family behind, in order to pass the message of General Howe's attack. She gave the message to her husband, a solider encamped at Whitemarsh, as Rebecca's father was.

The American Revolution seems like a long time ago. But as I write these words, some two hundred and fifty years later, I realize it's not that long ago at all. Our country is a relatively young one, and the actions of people who lived in Rebecca's time continue to shape our lives today.

The land I sit on right now was given to Continental soldiers after the war. The brand-new American government did not have enough money to pay the soldiers their promised wages.

Instead, the government bequeathed men—like Rebecca's father—acreage in the remote, tangled wilderness of the Ohio Valley. Those families traveled down the rivers, through the Appalachian Mountains, and settled here, clearing the forests and planting crops. As I wrote Rebecca's story, I was constantly reminded that here in my house, at my desk, I am perched on the bones of history.

The women behind Rebecca's story were real wives, mothers, and daughters. They were ordinary women who showed extraordinary courage in order to protect both the family members they loved and the ideals they believed in.

I hope you too will be inspired to stand up for the beliefs and people you love in ways big and small. I wish you all the courage Rebecca had when she rode alone through that frozen December night.

MAKING CONNECTIONS

1. Rebecca needs to be brave several times during this story. Look back through the text. Name three instances in which Rebecca specifically summons her bravery and explain how she does so.

2. Although readers are introduced to Rebecca's father several times in flashbacks throughout the story, he doesn't actually appear until the end of the book. Why would an author choose to include flashbacks, and what purpose do they serve? Use specific examples from this story to support your argument.

3. The story revolves around Rebecca's decision to carry the message to her father. Think back to a time when you had to make a difficult decision. What was the situation, and what did you decide? How was your own decision-making process the same as or different from Rebecca's?

GLOSSARY

bog (BOG)—a type of wetland that includes wet, spongy ground and pools of muddy water

clove hitch (klohv hich)—a knot securing a rope temporarily to an object; it consists of a turn around the object, over the standing part, around the object again, and under the last turn

commence (kuh-MENS)—to begin

congenial (kuhn-JEEN-ee-yuhl)—pleasant and enjoyable

correspondence (kor-uh-SPON-dehns)—communication by means of letters

dispatch (dis-PACH)—an important official message

embankment (em-BANK-muhnt)—a raised edge or roadway that is built to carry a roadway or hold back water

encampment (en-KAMP-muhnt)—the place where a group (such as a body of troops) is camped

flint (FLINT)—a hard, gray rock that produces sparks when struck by metal

gait (GATE)—the manner in which a horse moves; gaits include the walk, trot, canter, and gallop

gelding (GEL-ding)—a male horse that can't be used for breeding

hysterical (hi-STER-i-kuhl)—emotionally violent and uncontrollable

impulse (IM-puhls)—a sudden, strong desire to do something

inscrutable (in-SKROO-tuh-buhl)—difficult to understand

meager (MEE-ger)—very small or too small in amount

parlor (PAHR-lur)—a formal living room

Patriot (PAY-tree-uht)—a person who sided with the colonies during the Revolutionary War

peat (PEET)—partly decayed plant matter found in bogs and swamps

pious (PAHY-uhs)—deeply religious

Quaker (KWAY-kur)—a member of the Religious Society of Friends, a group founded in the 1600s, who prefers simple religious services and opposes war

Redcoat (RED-koht)—British soldier, named after the color of his uniform

regiment (REJ-uh-muhnt)—a large group of soldiers who fight together as a unit

sentry (SEN-tree)—a guard

spasm (SPAZ-uhm)—a sudden tightening of a muscle that cannot be controlled

Tories (TOHR-eez)—colonists who remained loyal to the British government

vivid (VIV-id)—sharp and clear

ABOUT THE AUTHOR

Emma Carlson Berne has written many volumes
of historical fiction for young people, including the
Girls Survive title *Ruth and the Night of Broken Glass:
A WWII Survival Story*. She lives in Cincinnati, Ohio,
with her husband and three little boys.